# FORWARD

Isn't a campfire the perfect place to tell stories? Particularly stories that keep you in suspense imagining all kinds of different outcomes. Sometimes there is a life lesson involved but more often than not, campfire stories are just a reflection of someone's imagination on steroids.

My Dad loved to tell stories particularly about the "wild west." They'd always end with him overcoming great odds to become the hero. So there is a legacy of story telling in my family.

Now imagine you are in front of a blazing campfire with family and friends and listen to the following six stories that I have made up which involve each of my very special grandkids: Will, Nolan, Maddie, Emily, Ally and Tyler.

I hope you enjoy each story as my Grandkids said they did. Remember they are not literary masterpieces by any stretch of the imagination. They are simply meant to entertain a bunch of kids sitting around a campfire, and yes, I believe the adults present will get a kick out of them too. So read them with gusto and as you do, don't forget to have a yummy S'More to make the event even more enjoyable.

Bruce Hobbs

# TABLE OF CONTENTS

# A NIGHT AT SNAKE POINT

Schools out Yes!!! Will turns to his Mom and asks, "Are we going to the lake this summer?"

"I don't know Will, your Dad hasn't made any reservations because he's trying to wrap up an important land deal." Will shrugs his shoulders and goes back to playing Black Ops II, his favorite game on his Xbox 360.

When they pull into their driveway there is Will's Dad beaming from ear to ear waving a piece of paper.

"We did it, we did it!" he exclaims as Will and his Mom leave the car.

"Did what?" asks Will.

"We struck a deal this morning," giving Will a high five.

"Are we rich now?" Will responds with great expectation.

"No, no, no, but it means we might now be able to spend a few days at the lake after all!"

After making several calls, Will's Dad finally finds a place to rent at the lake. Hearing the news, Will's entire family is overjoyed, as Great Pond is their most favorite lake in all of Maine for a vacation.

The car is jammed full: Will, his dog "Fozzie", a mutt whose piercing bark could shatter glass, his sister Maddie, brother Tyler and his Mom and Dad.

"Sorry for the late start his Dad says, as the rain pelts the windshield making the lights from oncoming cars seem like movable flashlights searching for objects in the dark. We're almost there. Belgrade Lakes Village is only five miles from here and that's where we pick up keys to the camp. Sorry I couldn't get the place we've rented in past years but this one was the only one available on the entire lake."

"Where is this place?" Will asks.

"It's on Snake Point, across the lake from where we usually stay."

"Snake Point! Will screeches. Are there really snakes there?"

"Naw," his Dad says, "I believe they call it Snake Point because of its crooked shape. Don't worry Will, even if there were snakes there, if one bit you it would die instantly!"

"Right on Dad," Tyler pipes up from the back seat.

But Will's Dad's explanation isn't what some "old timers" say about Snake Point. They recall it as the place where a recluse old hermit lived for many years raising a variety of poisonous snakes, which reflected his rather bizarre religious beliefs, as well as his intention to keep away pesky "Flatlanders" who vacationed on the point each summer. In fact, he was nicknamed "Snake Man" by these old timers.

Since the death of "Snake Man", strange things seem to happen to renters of his large but somewhat dilapidated camp located at the tip of Snake Point. As a result, this rental property remained mostly vacant summer after summer despite the most enterprising efforts of local realtors. But occasionally, a latecomer, like Will's Dad, would come along and rent it out of sheer desperation.

"Where is this place? asks Will. We've been following this dirt road forever and I haven't seen a single camp for miles."

"Patience, Will, I can't go any faster, as I can barely see the road with all this rain."

Just then the faint image of an out building comes into view, followed by another, and then there it is, Snake Man's camp, an old two story structure with a wrap around porch.

"Here we are," Will's Dad says, which went almost unnoticed by everyone except Will because they were all either texting on their iPhones or nodding off as it was nearly midnight.

The rain lets up a bit as they all rush from the car to the porch.

"Take only what you need to sleep in Will's Dad says. We'll unload the car in the morning."

"Where are the lights?" Will asks.

"Here Dad, use my cell phone flashlight," says Maddie.

"Wow, this place is creepy," Will exclaims after the lights come on.

"Let's put the perishables in the fridge," says Will's Mom.

As they put things away, they see a note on the kitchen table left by the Realtor welcoming them but citing a word of caution. "Don't go down into the cellar after dark. The light has been removed and besides there's nothing down there you will need anyway."

Of course that is all Will needs to hear as he immediately opens the cellar door.

His Dad shouts, "Will shut that damn door and stay out of the cellar and that goes for all of you as well."

With that they all grab their overnight bags and head upstairs to bed.

Will and Tyler share a bedroom, Maddie has her own and of course the master bedroom, is claimed by Will's parents.

By now it is well after midnight and after a hasty tooth brushing, everyone crashes.

"Tyler, Tyler you awake?" asks Will.

"Now I am," Tyler says sarcastically.

"Do you hear that scraping noise, it sounds as if it's coming from inside the wall."

"Knock it off Will, it's only your hyper-imagination kicking in. Shut up and go to sleep!"

Will rolls over and closes his eyes.

Moments later Will hears the noise again. Oh my God it's surreal. *I know there is something inside the wall next to me. But then he rationalizes it is probably a squirrel or something else seeking shelter from the rain.*

But a second trip to the bathroom reveals something else. As Will walks down the hall he hears the same noise and it seems to intensify as he approaches the stairs. He is surrounded by this strange scrapping sound, like tree branches rubbing against a tin roof but it is coming from inside the walls. *What could it be?*

Will returns to his room to get Tyler to help him investigate this mystery but when he gets rebuffed, he grabs Tyler's iPhone and decides to look into it himself.

As he approaches the stairs the noise gets louder. He activates the iPhone's flashlight and that's when he sees a shadow of something racing across the foot of the stairs below.

He slowly descends the creaky stairs and when he reaches the bottom he catches a glimpse of something racing across the floor into the kitchen. He proceeds cautiously until he finds himself in front of the cellar door.

At that moment the strange scratching noise stops. It is absolutely quiet.

Will pauses at the cellar door. He recalls the note on the kitchen table but his curiosity gets the better of him, so Will being Will, screws up his courage, opens the door and descends the stairs into the darkness below.

After reaching the cellar floor, Will can hardly see anything even with his iPhone flashlight. He looks for a light but as the Realtor had said, there is none. But there in the corner, next to what appears to be a trap door, he sees a wooden pole with a cloth wrapped around its end. It has been burned so Will concludes immediately it is a torch.

"Aha, I have my light source," he exclaims.

On a workbench nearby Will sees some matches and a gallon tin can of kerosene. He soaks the cloth with kerosene, lights it with a match and..."Voila" every inch of the cavernous cellar is visible.

He puts the kerosene tin on the floor and as he does he notices a trap door in the floor in front of him, which is almost indistinguishable because of all the junk strewn around it. He notices that it has a lock through the hasp but a closer look reveals the lock is not engaged. Will removes the lock and cautiously opens the trap door.

"Oh my God!" he cries out as the light from his flaming torch reveals hundreds of snakes: rattlesnakes, coral snakes, cottonmouths, and other varieties Will had never seen before.

The light clearly spooks the snakes, which sets off a hissing frenzy, and many start to scatter. A large rattler coils and strikes viciously at Will's foot. Will jumps back dropping the torch and knocks over the can of kerosene. When the flames from the torch ignite the kerosene, the whole cellar becomes an instant inferno.

Will dashes frantically up the stairs followed by an army of reptiles.

Will shouts out at the top of his lungs, "Mom, Dad, Maddie, Tyler, get out! Get out! Hurry! Hurry!"

Then Will feels someone shaking him violently.

"Wake up, Will, wake up, says Tyler! It's in the middle of the night and your ranting will wake up everyone!"

Will looks at the wad of blankets at the foot of his bed and realizes that what he has just experienced was only a bad dream. *Wow he thinks to himself, I can't believe it. It seemed so real!*

That evening in front of the campfire, Will's Dad asks, "Anyone got a good story to tell?"

Before anyone can reply, Will shouts out, you becha! I've got one even Tyler will like!

# I CAN, CAN'T I

Nolan loves baseball. Why not, he comes from a long line of baseball players. His great grandfather played for the "Bleeker Dutchmen," a talented semi pro team that played in the '40s. His grandfather played baseball in the 60s and could have played for the Phillies if Uncle Sam hadn't drafted him. And his Dad played high school baseball and currently coaches his little league baseball team. One thing they all had in common, they were pitchers!

So is it any wonder that Nolan, whose namesake is Nolan Ryan, a famous Hall of Fame pitcher, wants more than anything to be a pitcher on his little league team. There is one problem. When he tried out for the team, he just couldn't get the ball over the plate, so his father, the coach, had to tell him, "If you can't throw strikes, you can't pitch!"
As a result, Nolan was relegated to playing the outfield for that entire season as he had a wickedly strong arm. But the dream of becoming a pitcher simmered inside him for that entire season.

At last, the long winter ends. Winters in Maine seem to last forever but now that spring has finally arrived, Nolan and his backyard buddies, hit the sandlot near his home to play baseball. After all, his little league team had tryouts in just two weeks.

As Nolan heads home from the sandlot, he plays catch with his next-door buddy, Alex. When he tosses the ball wildly over Alex's head it lands in the front yard of a house nearby.

Alex says, "You get it, I gotta go," as he dashes off leaving Nolan all alone.

As Nolan retrieves his ball, he notices an old man rocking slowly back and forth on the porch.

"You play ball, kid?" the old man asks.

Nolan is startled by the question and is reluctant to say anything because he has been warned many times not to talk to strangers. But feeling like he should say something, he blurts out, "Yep," fetches his ball, and runs off.

The next day, after playing ball most of the afternoon, Nolan passes by the old man's house and there he is once again rocking back and forth on the porch.

"You like pitching?" the old man inquires.

"Yes sir," Nolan replies, surprised that he could even muster a reply.

"Looks like you got a pretty good fastball, the old man says with a smile. Need to get it over the plate though."

"Yea I know," Nolan replies as he dashes off.

The next time Nolan passes the old man's house, he is raking his lawn.

The old man says "Doing anything about your control?"

"Like what?" Nolan asks.

"Well many years ago when I pitched, I had a coach tell me that good control came from your head not your arm."

"Don't get it," says Nolan.

"Neither did I then, until the coach told me about the 3 C's."

"What's that?"

"Concentration, Control, Confidence, the old man says. You see when your eyes are fixed on the target or where you want the pitch to end up, your brain sends a signal to the muscles in your body that helps direct the ball to the place you are concentrating on. So concentration leads to control which in turn leads to gaining confidence and the whole cycle is repeated over and over"

"Wow, it sounds complicated!"

"Not really, the old man responds, it worked for me."

"It did?"

"Yes I was a pitcher once."

"Who'd you play for?"

"The New York Giants," the old man responds.

"You did?"

"Yes, but that was a long time ago."

Then the old man says, "Isn't it about time we introduced ourselves? What's your name?"

"My name is Nolan, what's yours?"

"Hal Schumacker, replies the old man, but please just call me Hal."

"Gotta go," Nolan says "see you tomorrow," and he dashes off.


After supper, Nolan uses his Mom's IMac to Google Hal Schumacker. *By God, Nolan exclaims as he opens the Giants' historical website, he's telling the truth!* Hal, or "Prince Hal" as he was referred to by his teammates, played for the Giants in the thirties and forties and in fact he was selected to play in the first All Star Game representing the National League.  He won several World Series games, nearly made the Baseball Hall of Fame, and he even struck out Babe Ruth. *Nolan couldn't wait to talk to the old man, or "Prince Hal," after playing ball the next day.*

Hal and Nolan become fast friends. They spend the next few days simply talking baseball and Nolan hears all about what it is like to play in the Majors.

The day before the spring tryouts Nolan screws up his courage and pops the big question.

Hal, "What can I do to make the team as a pitcher?"

Hal responds, "Remember the three C's."

"But I've tried to and it doesn't seem to work."

Hall gets up and goes into the house and returns with a small bottle filled with a liquid.

Hal says, "Each night before you pitch, take a sip of this and it may help. It helped me when I was struggling with control."

Noland goes home and stows the bottle under his mattress. That night he lay awake thinking, what if this stuff makes me sick and I miss the tryouts tomorrow. But before he dozes off he decides to take a chance, takes a swig from the bottle, and falls fast sleep.

At the tryouts the next day, his father calls out "Nolan it's your turn to pitch."

*As he takes the mound Nolan's legs feel weak and his stomach feels like his breakfast will retrace its previous path.*

Nolan winds up, and proceeds to throw the ball on the wrong side of the batter sending him diving into the dirt. *O my god, nothing has changed he thought.*

*Then Nolan suddenly feels a strange calm come over him as he concentrates very hard on the catcher's mitt.* The next pitch is a blazing fastball that crosses the plate as the coach yells...."Steeerike!" The following pitches also hit their mark, and after striking out six batters, his Dad says, "Great job, Nolan, you're the starter for our first game tomorrow."

That night, Nolan takes another swig of the liquid before falling asleep and sure enough it seems to work again as he pitches a one hitter and his team wins 6-1.

The season passes quickly after that and Nolan pitches extremely well, helping his team win the Northeastern Little League regional playoff, thereby earning them a chance to go to

Williamsport, Pennsylvania to compete in the Little League World Series.

After his team receives the formal invitation to go to Williamsport, he can't wait to tell Hal. He too has a chance to pitch in a World Series.

When he knocks on Hal's door, a passing neighbor calls out, "That won't do you much good, boy. Saw an ambulance rush Hal to the hospital yesterday."

Nolan is crushed by the news but he gets on his bike and makes fast tracks to the hospital.

When he enters the hospital he asks the receptionist if he could visit Hal Schumacher.

The receptionist says, "Are you part of his family?"

"No, he's just my friend."

"Then I'm afraid you can't see him as only family members are allowed to visit patients in the Intensive Care Unit."

Just then Nolan feels a hand on his shoulder and a soft voice says, "How do you know Hal?"

Nolan quickly recounts his past encounters with Hal and the woman takes his hand and heads for the elevator.

"Hal is my grandfather and I know he'd like to see you," she said.

When they enter Hal's room he lay on his bed appearing to be asleep and is covered with tubes and monitors that are tracking his vital signs.

Suddenly, Hal's eyes open. When he sees Nolan a slight smile crosses his face. In a somewhat garbled voice he says, "throwing any strikes these days?"

Nolan says enthusiastically, "Yes sir" and fills him in on the entire season.

"Sounds like you learned your three Cs all right," says Hal.

"I don't think it was that Hal," Nolan replies. I think it was the special stuff you gave me to take each night before I pitched." By the way, I'm almost out of it!

"Are you kidding kid, Hal says. Do you know what is in that bottle?"

"Nope," Nolan replies.

"That was nothing but sugar water; nothing magic about that stuff! What you lacked was confidence in yourself and that comes from self discipline, good concentration and control of your pitches."

Hal continues, "Remember Nolan, always concentrate on what's really important when you're playing ball and know that solutions to most problems come from within yourself. Have confidence in your abilities my friend!"

Nolan thanks Hal for his advice, gives him a big hug and leaves the room. As he does, he realizes that Hal's right. His pitching success was really only a matter of improving his concentration and gaining self-confidence. He had the ability all along. So he decides right then and there that when he faces future challenges, on or off the field, he will first say to himself: "I can, can't I!"

He hops on his bike and rides home knowing he is a very lucky boy to have a friend like Hal.

# THE NUTCRACKER

Maddie, short for Madeleine, loves to dance. In fact ballet dancing has taken up much of her time since the fifth grade. Now she is about to enter High school and she faces a dilemma. Three of her very best friends, who are also dancers, have decided to give up dancing to tryout for the school's cheerleading team. Of course all three are shoe-ins to make the team as ballet and modern dance training has made them both fit and agile which are important prerequisites for cheerleading.

But things are complicated by the fact that because her friends are no longer dancing, this puts Maddie in a unique position to be the premiere ballerina in her high school dance group which makes it very likely she will be selected to dance the Sugar Plum Fairy in the Nutcracker a few months from now.

But Maddie still feels the pressure to give up dancing for cheerleading. After all, cheerleaders are much more popular among the boys! So Maddie ponders what to do.

One evening Maddies' Mom calls out to her as she is moping in her room. "Come join us for a movie Maddie."

"We're leaving in an hour." her Dad adds, "I think you will really enjoy the film."

"What's it called?" Maddie asks.

"Mao's Last Dancer," her Dad replies.

"What's it about?"

"It's about a small boy who is plucked from a small Chinese village to become a ballet dancer and eventually he becomes the principal dancer at the Houston Ballet. It's a true story!"

"Sounds interesting," Maddie replies, as she descends the stairs to join her parents.

Maddie finds the movie mesmerizing. The dancing is superb, and the story is truly inspiring which leads her right then and there to decide to stick with dancing.

The risks the Chinese dancer took to do what he truly loved to do paled in comparison to the superficial risks Maddie faced of losing her best friends if she continues to dance. So she sets her goal on dancing the lead role in the upcoming performance of the Nutcracker.

Dancing is hard work. Yes, you need to have talent but above all, you have to be really dedicated and prepared to work very hard. Of course, it helps to have some good luck thrown in.

Maddie enters the competition for the lead in the Nutcracker and got it. But dancing the part of the Sugar Plum Fairy requires a much higher level of dancing skill than she is used to. Nevertheless she is determined to put in the extra time and effort to take full advantage of this unique opportunity.

The extra effort pays off but takes its toll on Maddie's body, especially on her left ankle that she had severely sprained while water skiing last summer. The injury has plagued her off and on since then, but particularly now as she prepares for her new role. At times, she would simply have to stop in the middle of a dance routine to "ice up" to relieve the pain.

Opening night is approaching and she desperately needs a new pair of ballet pointe shoes. *Can't dance the lead role in these old messed up ones she thinks to herself.*

In town there is only one place to buy dancing apparel and that is at Chez Versailles.

When Maddie and her Mom enter the shop, the owner, Madame Veronique, greets them enthusiastically.

"Hi Maddie, understand you're dancing the lead in the Nutcracker?"

"Yes," Maddie replies, and I need a new pair of pointe shoes."

After trying on several pairs, the owner says, "that's all I have in your size."

*Oh no Maddie thinks, what am I going to do.*

At that moment a rather elegant older women appears who had over heard their conversation.

"You should try on these, my dear. They might fit you and they're already broken in," she says.

"Thanks," Maddie replies, and after putting them on she *thought, boy they fit perfectly and they are of top quality but I'd really prefer a new pair. Then on second thought, she realizes that she has no better solution.*

She thanks the women again, tucks the shoes under her arm and leaves the store for home.

The big night finally arrives. She takes her things backstage, dresses, puts on her borrowed pointe shoes for the first time, and begins to warm up. She notices right from the start that when she performs some of the more difficult movements, the pain in her ankle is gone

Then she hears the stage manager call, "Maddie you're up, take your position."

She peeks through the curtain and sees that the auditorium is packed. And there in the front row are her three dancing buddies. The butterflies rage inside her. This is her big moment.

As she dances, she feels no pain. Her moves are graceful and effortless. She feels she is in a zone that she has never experienced before. And then it all ends to a standing ovation and receiving a large bouquet of red roses from her jubilant parents.

Her dance instructor rushes up and gives her a hug and says, "Maddie I have never seen a high school student perform this role so beautifully."

And then Madame Veronique appears who also heaps praise on her for her performance.

Maddie asks Madame Veronique, "Who was that delightful lady who lent me her dance shoes?"

"Oh she is Alexandra Ansanelli. She used to be a principal dancer with the New York City Ballet and at The Royal Ballet in London."

Maddie replies, "No kidding. I would really like to meet her again. By the way, do you think she would let me keep her shoes?"

"Yes Maddie, I'm sure she would! These are the pointe shoes Alexandra wore in her last performance before retiring from ballet a year ago and she brought them to the shop for me to give them to someone who could use them. How about it if I arrange for you to meet Alexandra and judging from your performance tonight, you two have lots to talk about."

Maddie is elated. She thanks Madame Veronique profusely and gives her a big hug. *As she does she thinks to herself, something magical happened tonight wearing Alexandra's shoes. The energy I had and no pain, wow! I guess everyone deserves a little magic in his or her life once in a while. I certainly got more than my share tonight!*

*Maddie picks up her shoes, and leaves the theater thinking she is the luckiest girl in the world.*

# THE BATTLE OF FAIRY ISLAND

Emily loves to spend time at her grandparent's camp on a lake in Maine. She likes it particularly when Margaret, her best friend, accompanies her and they sleep in the one room bunkhouse next to the camp.

On this particular day at camp, they spend the entire afternoon building a "fairy house" next to the water's edge.

A fairy house, according to Emily's specifications, must consist of many pieces of driftwood assembled in the shape of a lean to, garnished with many flowers or anything else of color. Obviously, any good fairy is very particular when it comes to a place to live requiring very exacting standards. Finally they finish their construction project and it is time for bed.

Emily wakes up in the middle of the night and needs to go to the bathroom in the main camp.

On her return she notices a strange white light coming from the fairy house they had just constructed. She races to tell Margaret whom she wakes up and they both go to check out this strange sight.

As they get near the fairy house Emily says, "Do you see it?"

"See what?" says Margaret.

"The light."

"There's no light," Margret replies curtly, and dashes back to the bunkhouse.

Emily just stands there amazed as she can clearly see the light, so she goes closer to check it out. As she approaches the fairy house, the light brightens. Then she gets close enough to see that the light is coming from the tip of what looks to be a wand held by a miniature figure with tiny wings. Emily thinks to herself, wow is this what fairies look like. They are so small!

"Hi," says the fairy, which really spooks Emily, but she responds,

"Who are you?"

"I am the Queen Fairy of Fairy Island and I came upon your fairy house as I was escaping from the wicked Dark Fairy who attacked and conquered my island with her army of grasshoppers."

"Where is your island?" Emily asks.

"Over there," the Fairy points.

"That's Hoyt Island," says Emily.

"I know, but that's where all the fairies live who are from around here."

"Oh," Emily replies, "Is there anything I can do to help?"

The Queen Fairy thinks for a bit then says, "Yes I think you can. Do you believe in fairies?"

"I do now," replies Emily.

"Good, but you can't help me until you become the size of a fairy so you can fly with me to my island over there."

"OK," Emily says, as the Fair Queen sprinkles her with some kind of sparkling dust that instantly reduces her to the size of the Queen Fairy.

Emily looks around her and everything appears to be so large. A passing squirrel causes her nearly to panic as it looks like a charging buffalo.

"Don't worry," says the Fairy Queen, "I'll protect you but now that its daybreak, we need to fly over to the island to do battle with the Dark Fairy."

"I can't fly," says Emily.

"Of course you can says the Queen Fairy, You are now a fairy and all fairies can fly, so let's go" and they took off together.

As they approach the island, the Fairy Queen points out the home of the Dark Fairy.

"I can see why they call her the Dark Fairy," Emily says. "You can hardly see her house it's so dark."

"That's because it is surrounded by a horde of grasshoppers who protect her and serve as her army. She now controls the entire island and holds my subjects as prisoners."

They land in a remote area far enough away from the Dark Fairy's house so as to be safe while they make their plans and when they are finished, they take off to challenge the Dark Fairy and her army of grasshoppers.

As they approached the Dark Fairy's house, Emily looks up and sees the first grasshopper. *Wow, it's the size of a bald eagle and really scary looking,* Emily thinks.

Just then a grasshopper spots them and sounds the alarm. It takes only seconds for the word to spread. *Hundreds of grasshoppers make enough noise to practically pierce you eardrums, Emily says to herself.* And then they all attack.

As they approach, the Fairy Queen dips into her bag of fairy dust again and sprinkles it over Emily who instantly returns to her normal size. Emily quickly tears off a large branch of a nearby tree and begins swatting the attacking grasshoppers. It doesn't take long for the grasshoppers to realize that they have no chance against Emily. They retreat and depart the island, leaving the Dark Fairy without protection.

Just then the Dark Fairy appears and says, "You have won this time but someday I'll return to reclaim this place."

The Fairy Queen responds emphatically, "Oh no you won't, not as long as I have people like Emily on my side!"

The Dark Fairy grunts something as she flies away. And as she does, Emily notices that the entire area begins to light up.

"What's going on?" Emily asks.

"My subjects are returning to their houses now that they no longer have to fear the Dark Fairy," the Queen Fairy says.

The Fairy Queen does her magic once again and she and Emily fly off together across the lake to Emily's fairy house. When Emily has been restored to her normal size, she asks the Queen Fairy, "Will you be leaving now?"

"Yes, Emily, I only came here to escape the Dark Fairy and thanks to you and your belief in fairies, I can now return to rule Fairy Island.

You know Emily, it takes very special person to believe in something they haven't actually seen or experienced before. Some say seeing is believing.  But I say, sometimes believing is seeing." With that the Queen Fairy flies off and disappears.

Just then Emily hears her Father shout "breakfast is ready."

Emily realizes that she is starved as she dashes off to find Margaret. *As she does, she thinks to herself, what shall I tell her about winning the battle of Fairy Island? I know she wouldn't believe me anyway, so I guess some things are better left unsaid. She smiles, and then says to herself,  but am I glad I believe in Fairies!*

# A HELPING HAND

School is out and now Ally has plenty of free time on her hands. When she does, she loves to simply hang out in her room reading, watching TV, or texting her friends.

As evening approaches, her Mom calls from downstairs, "Ally we are all going to the movies, want to join us?"

"No," Ally says which is the kind of reply many parents get from a reluctant teenager. "Just go, I'll be fine!" she shouts.

Her family took off and at last she is alone in her castle, a bedroom awash with books, magazines, and a pile of cloths waiting for the laundry. She savors an evening like this as she turns on her TV to watch one of her favorite programs.

It wasn't long that Ally hears a noise downstairs. Sounds like glass shattering. Then she hears voices.

She leaves her room and peers downstairs and even though it was dark now, she could see the silhouettes of two men removing their 46-inch TV from the wall. One of the men heads for the stairs and Ally dashes back to her room and covers her with all the dirty laundry she could find.

When the intruder opens the door to her room, he yells to his mate, check out this mess!

Ally holds her breath but she is sure her pounding heart would give her away. Then the sneeze comes after what seems like an eternity of trying to hold it back.

Hearing it, the intruder uncovers the mound of cloths covering her and says, "Well, what do we have here!"

He calls his partner who enters the room and inquires, "What do we do with her? She's seen our faces and you know what that means!"

"Tie her up," the other intruder says harshly. Put her in the trunk and let's get outta here! We'll decide what to do with her when we get back to our place."

They tie her hands behind her, put her in the trunk of their car and take off.

*Wow Ally thought, it is really cramped in here. Can't see a thing!*

But while she was frightened out of her wits, she didn't panic. She remembers that she has her new iPhone in her pocket, but she couldn't remember whether it was charged.

And then she feels a cold clammy something grab her foot, scamper up her leg to the small of her back close to where her hands are tied. Whatever it was it started tugging vigorously on the ropes that bound her wrist. What is this thing! Whatever it is it loosens the ropes at least to the point where Ally can begin to move her hands. She pulls and twists her hands and wrists as hard as she can and suddenly the ropes slip over them.

Ally reaches into her pocket for her IPhone. Thank God it is charged! Her next thought is to dial 911 but when she does she finds that there is no signal. She searches for the flashlight app and when she turns on the light it hurts her eyes but they adjust quickly.

Then she sees it. "Oh My God!" she screams, as she observes a large bloodied hand, severed just above the wrist, lying by her feet.

The car comes to an abrupt stop. What's next she thought; are they now coming to get me? She recalls all the movies she has seen where terrible things happen to victims of a kidnapping. She starts to whimper, and then come the sobs.

*Oh how I wish I had gone to the movies with my family tonight she mutters to herself.*

She hears voices but they become faint and no one comes to get her, at least not yet. She is left in a dark trunk with a severed hand and she has no idea where she is.

After several minutes, Ally recalls from one of the many high dramas she has watched that a captive in a similar situation had punched out the rear taillight to try to get someone's attention. So she pulls out the wires attaching the taillight and begins kicking the back of it.

After several hard whacks, it finally pops out. She peers through the hole but could barely see anything because it is dark outside. However, she could see enough to know that she was in a wooded area and the faint recurring sound of a foghorn suggests that she is near a body of water.

Then a weird thing happened. The hand, that had been dormant, began to quiver. It gets up on its fingertips and moves toward the taillight. Ally let out a scream, as the hand climbs over her and pauses before the taillight opening as if it is considering what to do, then it quickly slips through the narrow opening and disappears.

Moments later, the trunk lid pops open. Ally wastes no time getting out and there on the ground lay the hand, seemly waiting for Ally to appear. In disbelief, Ally takes out her iPhone and takes a picture of it to be sure she isn't hallucinating.  All of a sudden the hand springs up and dashes towards an old shed nearby.

Ally scans the area for her captors. She continues to hear muffled voices coming from the shed so she quietly closes the trunk and takes off towards the woods, using her IPhone flashlight sparingly not wanting to attract attention.

It doesn't take long for her to realize that she is on an island as she comes to the water's edge and observes a bridge to the mainland and some lights on a distant shore about a mile away.

She knows that if she follows the road and uses the bridge, that would be the first place her captors would look, so she decides to make the swim, after all, she is one of the best freestyle swimmers on her high school swim team.

The water is freezing as it is throughout Maine in May.
It isn't swimming the distance Ally worries about, but it is the cold water that really scares her. But she plunges in and begins swimming.

As she swims, she thinks about anything that helps to keep her from losing consciousness. But it wasn't long before her leg cramps up and swimming against the current saps her strength. *I just can't make it she thinks to herself. Oh how I'll miss my parents, and yes, even my brother and sister.*

As she was about to pass out, her foot strikes a sharp rock. "Ouch," she cries out, but her legs were so numb from the cold water that she could barely stand up and steady herself on the big rock beneath her feet.

She removes her IPhone from her pocket, thinking how glad she was to have purchased the waterproof case against the strong objections of her Dad.

When she turns on the light she notices a chained buoy nearby which says "Beware of Rocks." She could barely remain standing because of the current when she sees the running lights of a small motorboat coming in her direction. She waves frantically while shining her light to attract the boat. Yes! The fisherman sees her, changes course and comes to help her. He pulls her into his boat and says, "What the heck are you doing out here?"

Ally replies, "It's a long story," which she relates to him as they head to his house on the mainland.

When they get there, Ally couldn't stop shivering but the quilt blanket and hot tea helps to restore her senses.

When the police arrive she is fine and gives them a full account of what happened, minus the severed hand part that she knew they would not believe anyway, and then they all set out to find the shed on the island.

It doesn't take long since the shed is close to the road, the only one on the small island and it is close to the bridge. The police surround the shed and they nab the two kidnappers without a struggle.

When they all go behind the shed, they come across a body with a severed arm. And there resting on its chest is the bloodied hand.

"How gross" exclaims the policeman!

*Amazing, Ally thinks to herself, realizing now that the hand had only been on a quest searching for its rightful place and had finally found it.*

Then one of the kidnappers says to Ally, "Hey kid, how did you get out of the trunk?"

Ally responds with a wry smile, "Oh I just had a very clever 'helping hand' assist me!"

"What?" said the kidnapper, who had no idea of what she meant.

Then Ally remembers the picture of the hand she had taken on her iPhone. Now that she realizes it wasn't a hallucination after all, she decides that the "helping hand" was to be her little secret that no one else ever needed to know. Besides, no one would ever believe her account of what happened, even if they saw the picture.

She smiles, as she deletes the picture, puts her IPhone in her pocket, and gets into the policeman's car to go home. *What a night she thinks, what a night!*

# THE WEST RIVER HUNT

Tyler hangs up the phone elated. His grandfather has just invited him to go on a deer hunt and his parents have given their permission. How cool is that!  Hunting and fishing are among his most favorite things to do, besides playing golf of course. To be honest, it isn't the hunting he liked so much, that is hard work. But being with his grandfather and his cronies at the West River Camp is always special. There he plays poker, eats great meals and hears all kinds of wild stories especially about his great grandfather or 'Grampie' the name Tyler gave him.

But before going further, you need to know something the West River House. It is a hunting camp located on 18 acres in the lower Adirondack Mountains of upstate New York. Tyler's great grandfather father and his friends built it in the late fifties and it is very close to West River from which it gets its name. Despite its sparse amenities, Tyler loves its simplicity and the fond memories of the good times he has had there.

Tyler lands in Albany and his grandfather picks him up at the airport. They go directly to camp hoping to arrive in time for cocktail hour. On arrival, everyone gives Tyler a warm welcome. They make it a special point to emphasize how much he has grown since they last saw him. Tyler winches at all this attention, but recognizes that's just what older folks do and it didn't really matter anyway because he was just glad to be in their company.

The hunt the next day starts early. Everyone packs a lunch and Tyler's grandfather gives him a candy bar to have after the hunt. He also reminds him to pack his raincoat, compass, and hunting knife and to take some matches, as he hands him his rife and six shells.

Tyler decides not to take his raincoat when he observes the sun beginning to rise with not a cloud in the sky. One less thing to carry he thinks, so he stuffs the raincoat under his bunk and leaves.

They all cross West River by boat and all twelve hunters gather together on the riverbank to plan their first drive.

Tyler has been on a deer drive before which is where the hunters divide in half with one group called "watchers", heading in one direction to sit and wait while the "drivers" set out from the opposite direction to drive the deer toward them while making loud yelping sounds referred to as "barking".

Driving is hard work and the young hunters usually get the lion's share of driving. So his grandfather turns to Tyler and says, "You are on the first drive. Stay in hearing distance of the other drivers and above all don't stray too far to the left where there is a densely wooded swap bog with lots of scrub brush. It's an area where you can easily get lost."

"Yeah, I know," he replies, vaguely recalling the area from past hunts.

It wasn't twenty minutes into the drive when Tyler hears three gunshots. Usually three shots in close succession mean someone has bagged their buck. He stops barking, as did the other drivers because deer if they're not hit would be startled by the gunfire, and will often double back and head to the drivers who might then get a shot.

That's exactly what happens in this case. Just as Tyler positions himself between a couple of scrub pines to get a better view, he hears someone yell, "Here he comes!"
And within minutes there appears a large eight- point buck heading directly towards Tyler.

Tyler freezes and when the deer sees him raise his rifle, he veers sharply to Tyler's left toward the swamp bog.

Tyler's heart races as he lowers his rifle and makes chase. The big buck is easy to follow because his tracks are so fresh and distinct. *Tyler thinks if I could only bag him he'd be the "talk of the camp" for the entire weekend.*

The going is tough as the swap bog is thick with downed and rotting timber dotted with small scrub evergreens. But he keeps following the deer's trail deeper and deeper into the bog until he loses sight of the deer's tracks altogether.

Tyler decides to quite tracking the deer but finds himself in thick bush so he keeps walking to find a clearing where he might get his bearings.

When he finally reaches an opening, he scans the area but recognizes nothing.

*"Oh my God he says to himself, I'm lost!"*

He sits down and tries not to panic but then the tears come followed by muffled sobs.

*"Why did I follow that damn deer," he said to himself. "I should have known better."*

It is now mid afternoon when he sees someone in the distance approaching him. He is an older man and as he approaches he says to Tyler, "You lost kid?"

"Sure am," Tyler responds sheepishly.

But as Tyler gets a closer look at the man, he thinks he recognizes him. He looks like a younger version of his great grandfather "Grampie" who passed away in Florida a few years before. Yes, he looks exactly like the pictures of Grampie that were prominently displayed on the walls of the West River camp.

"Oh my God, is that you Grampie?" Tyler blurts out.

"Yep," the old man says, "That's me."

"But I thought you were...," he pauses...

 Grampie breaks the silence by saying,
"I'd suggest you stop walking and stay put if you don't know where you're going!"

Tyler explains the circumstances surrounding his dilemma and Grampie replies, "I know, it happens to the best of us sometimes. But now it's time for you to use your head. I suggest you fire three shots cause I'm sure the guys are looking for you right now and it will give them an indication of where you are."

Tyler puts a bullet in the chamber and fires a shot, then another, followed by another. They wait but hear nothing.

By now it is mid-afternoon and it turns cold and begins to rain.

"Where's your raingear?" Grampie asks.

"I left it back at camp," Tyler says.

"That wasn't too smart," says Grampie.

*Oh why didn't I bring my raincoat, Tyler thought, how stupid!*

"You know Tyler, you always want to stay dry in the woods and that is why hunters always carry raingear and wear wool clothing. Wool absorbs a lot of moisture and traps in your body heat that helps keep you warm.

Then he asks Tyler for his hunting knife, and says, "Help me find a large birch tree which shouldn't be too difficult because birch trees are plentiful  throughout the Adirondacks."

"There's one!" Tyler yells.

Grampie approaches the tree and begins cutting its bark in a perfect circle. Then four feet below it he cuts another circle. Then he slices the bark in a straight line from the first circle to the bottom one and begins peeling off the bark around the tree and when he finishes it is one complete piece of birch bark in the shape of a poncho. He cuts a hole in the center and puts the birch bark poncho over Tyler's head and says,

"Now you have your raingear!"

*Wow Tyler thought, that's really neat.*

The rain continues so Tyler and Grampie collect all the birch bark they could find to start a fire. *Tyler remembers that birch bark burns even when it is wet because of its flammable composition.*

After collecting a pile of birch bark, they look for a place to make camp and built a fire.

Grampie says, "You're going to need plenty of wood to keep a fire burning all night."

So they gather as much firewood as they can before it gets dark.

As dusk settles in, they built a big fire and sit together in silence as they warm up.

Tyler takes out his sandwich and candy bar and devours them. Then just as he appeared, Grampie is gone. Tyler is now all alone.

It is shortly after dark when Tyler hears the first howl. It sounds far away but as time passes it gets closer. He knew that there are now coyotes in this region and with each howl he throws another piece of wood on the fire to discourage any of these persistent predators from getting closer.

Tyler is drowsy and doses off. When he awakes he sees four pair of red eyes glowing in the dark not far away. Moments later there are six, then sixteen.

*Oh my God, he thinks, I'm surrounded by coyotes!*

*He* fires off two shots and they disappear. But it wasn't long before they return. He has only one bullet left and that's when he really gets scared. *How do I survive the night with only one bullet and a pack of coyotes stalking me?*

It is often said that in such dire circumstances your entire life passes before you as it does for Tyler at that moment. *He thinks of all the things he really values, people mostly, and the things he has said or done that he'd like to take back, as well as the many things he still wants to do, like play pro golf.*

And then a charging coyote breaks his somber reflection; followed by another, and then another. He fires his last bullet at the leading animal and it went down and the others scattered.

He builds up the fire to frighten the other aggressors and searches for more torch material.

And then out of the woods spring two more coyotes. One grabs his foot as the other goes for his throat. As Tyler swings his rifle at one of the attacking beasts, two shots ring out and both coyotes collapse instantly at Tyler's feet.

Into the firelight Grampie appears with his rifle.

"Boy am I glad to see you" Tyler blurts out. "Where did you go after we started the fire?"

"Had to get my gun," Grampie replies and then without saying another word , he disappears again into the darkness.

Tyler is alone again but this time things are very different. No more howling as dawn approaches. With first light Tyler hears the echo of a rifle shot. Then another followed by another.

Tyler grabs several fistfuls of wet grass and throws them on the fire to make smoke. Soon he hears a faint voice yelling his name. He begins to shout and then he hears a voice say, "There he is, there he is!"

His grandfather rushes up and grabs him and gives him a huge bear hug that seems to last several minutes.

"God I'm glad to see you!" he says.

Tyler responds, "I'm OK and I'm sure glad you found me Papa!" "I'm so sorry for....."

His grandfather cut him off saying, "you're OK and that's all that matters! Now let's get back to camp."

"You bet," Tyler says since he just wants to get back there, clean up and get some sleep.

As they all walk out of the woods, Tyler is bombarded with all sorts of questions about his night in the woods. As he fields each of them, he deliberately leaves out the encounter with Grampie because he knows no one would believe him.

As he walks, he thinks how lucky he is to have survived the night and to have encountered a rejuvenated Grampie whom he knew only as a very old and frail man at the end of life. What he experienced that night confirmed all the great things he had heard about Grampie over the years. He also learned a lot about himself, lessons that he would treasure the rest of his life. He couldn't imagine that there would be any greater challenge he would face in life than what he had just experienced.

When he gets back to camp he cleans up, finds his bed, and crashes.

As he sleeps, Grampie reappears this time in his dream.

He says to Tyler, "Glad you made it out of the woods safely."

Tyler responds, "I'm sure glad to have had your help Grampie and boy you are a good shot!"

"Yeah, sometimes you get lucky, Grampie responds.

Thanks so much Grampie for being there when I really needed someone."

"Don't mention it, Grampie replies. Glad I could help. And Tyler, remember the lessons you learned in the woods with me and know that I'm never further away than your very next thought."

Then suddenly Tyler wakes up to a loud shout from the kitchen, "Come and get it."

He jumps out of bed and races downstairs for dinner. He is starved!

# EPILOGUE

I hope you have enjoyed these stories as much as I have enjoyed telling them. Each is as different as the grandkids who are depicted in each of them. I should emphasize that they bear no relationship to reality. They are simply a product of my imagination and are only intended to serve as a good yarn.

Tell these stories as written or embellish them anyway you wish, as their sole purpose is to entertain anyone who is willing to listen. Remember, any story is best told in front of a campfire. So start the fire and top off each story with a marshmallow, piece of Hersey's chocolate wedged between two graham crackers, toasted over the campfire, and remember to have one for me!

Bruce Hobbs (aka by my grandkids) Papa Goose

(Nolan, Emily, Maddie, Ally, Tyler, and Will)

Made in the USA
San Bernardino, CA
11 December 2014